PEOPLE IN MY NEIGHBORHOOD
STICKER BOOK

Anna Nilsen
illustrated by Sue Cony

Ask a grownup to help you take the sticker pages out
of the middle of the book so you can see the stickers
and the pictures side by side.

Turn to the first picture. Read one of the riddles and
find the sticker that answers it. Then peel off the sticker
and choose a place in the picture to put it. Keep
going until you have used all the stickers.
The answers are on page 16.

CANDLEWICK PRESS
CAMBRIDGE, MASSACHUSETTS

I'm the one with a hammer
and gray hair.
I'm fixing the window.
Who am I?

I have a big bag of mail
and a pair of blue pants.
I'm delivering a letter.
Who am I?

I'm the one dressed in red
with some bread in my hand.
I'm feeding the ducklings.
Who am I?

I'm wearing boots and holding a fork and a shovel. I'm planting some roses. Who am I?

I'm wearing a hat
and a green-and-white apron.
I'm selling bananas.
Who am I?

I'm trying on a hat
with a purple ribbon.
I'm doing the shopping.
Who am I?

I'm waiting for the train.
I have a dog, a purse,
and an umbrella.
Who am I?

LONDON

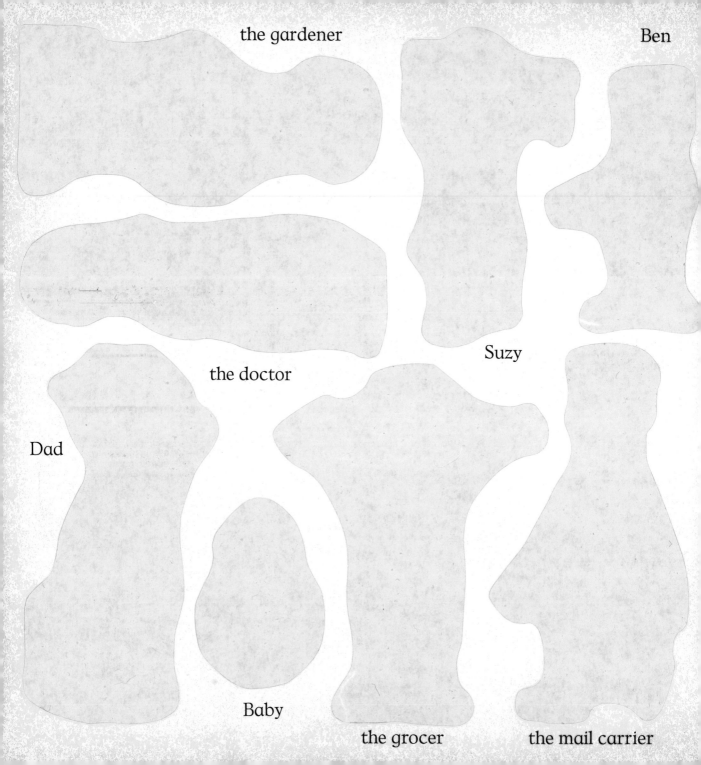

the gardener

Ben

the doctor

Suzy

Dad

Baby

the grocer

the mail carrier

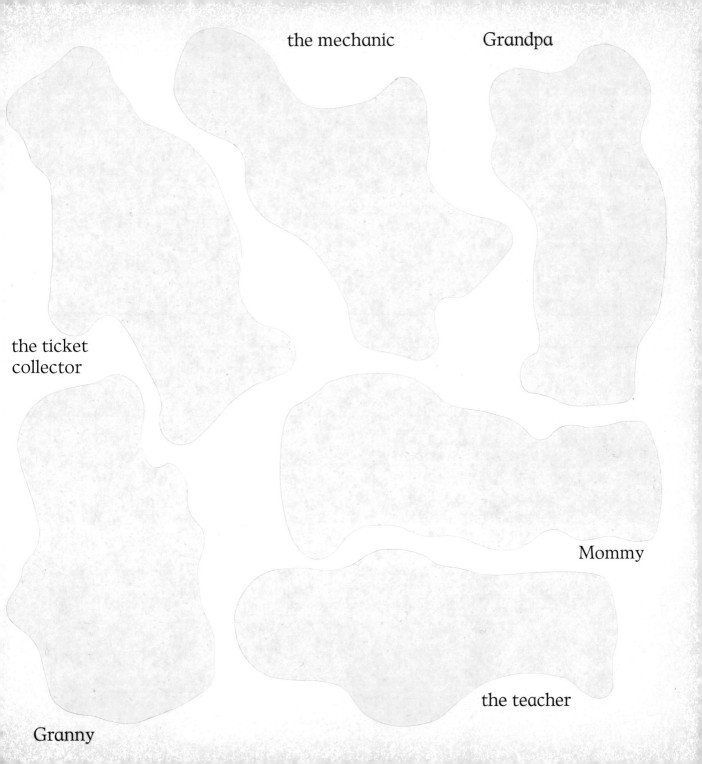

the mechanic

Grandpa

the ticket
collector

Mommy

the teacher

Granny

I have a black-and-gold cap
and a bushy mustache.
I'm collecting the tickets.
Who am I?

I'm the one dressed in brown and holding an oil can and a wrench. I'm fixing a truck. Who am I?

I'm washing my car
with a bucket and sponge.
My hair is short and curly.
Who am I?

I have paint on my face
and my hair is in two braids.
I'm painting a picture.
Who am I?

12

I'm reading a story
to a class full of children.
I'm wearing my glasses.
Who am I?

I'm playing with a rattle.
I'm dressed in light blue.
I giggle and gurgle.
Who am I?

In my heavy black bag
there are bottles and pills.
I make people better.
Who am I?

Answers

For Kerry
A. N.

For my dad
S. C.

Text copyright © 1994 by Anna Nilsen

Illustrations copyright © 1994 by Sue Cony

Second U.S. edition 1998

ISBN 0-7636-0430-5

2 4 6 8 10 9 7 5 3 1

Printed in Hong Kong

Candlewick Press
2067 Massachusetts Avenue
Cambridge, Massachusetts 02140